The
Giant's
Apprentice

ALSO BY MARGARET K. WETTERER

Patrick and the Fairy Thief
*illustrated by Enrico Arno*

The Mermaid's Cape
*illustrated by Elise Primavera*

(MARGARET K. MC ELDERRY BOOKS)

# The Giant's Apprentice

## Margaret K. Wetterer

*Illustrated by* **ELISE PRIMAVERA**

A Margaret K. Mc Elderry Book  Atheneum  1982  New York

For his technical advice, I would like to thank William Reichert, the Village Blacksmith of Northport, New York.

M.K.W.

LIBRARY OF CONGRESS CATALOGING IN PUBLICATION DATA

Wetterer, Margaret K.
   The giant's apprentice.

   "A Margaret E. McElderry book."
   Summary: Liam is apprenticed to his uncle, a skillful blacksmith and the finest storyteller in Ireland; when Liam disappears, the blacksmith must pit his wits and strength against a giant to save him.
   [1. Blacksmiths—Fiction.   2. Giants—Fiction.
3. Ireland—Fiction]   I. Primavera, Elise, ill.
II. Title.
PZ7.W533Gi    [E]    81-10810
ISBN 0-689-50229-X    AACR2

Text copyright © 1982 by Margaret K. Wetterer
Illustrations copyright © 1982 by Elise Primavera
Published simultaneously in Canada by McClelland & Stewart, Ltd.
Composition by Dix Typographers
Syracuse, New York
Printed by Halliday Lithograph Corporation
West Hanover, Massachusetts
Bound by A. Horowitz & Sons/Bookbinders
Fairfield, New Jersey
First Edition

*For my brother, Dr. Martin J. Kelly,
everyone's favorite uncle.*

M.K.W.

*For Dilys*

E.P.

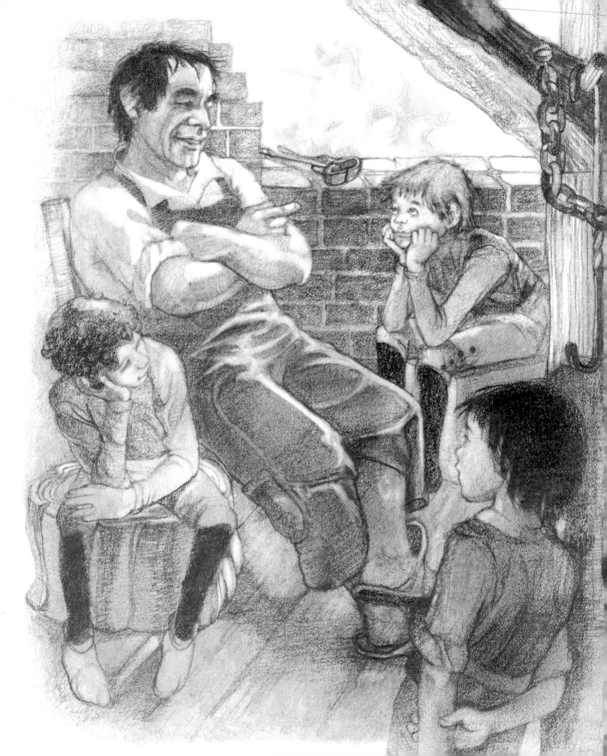

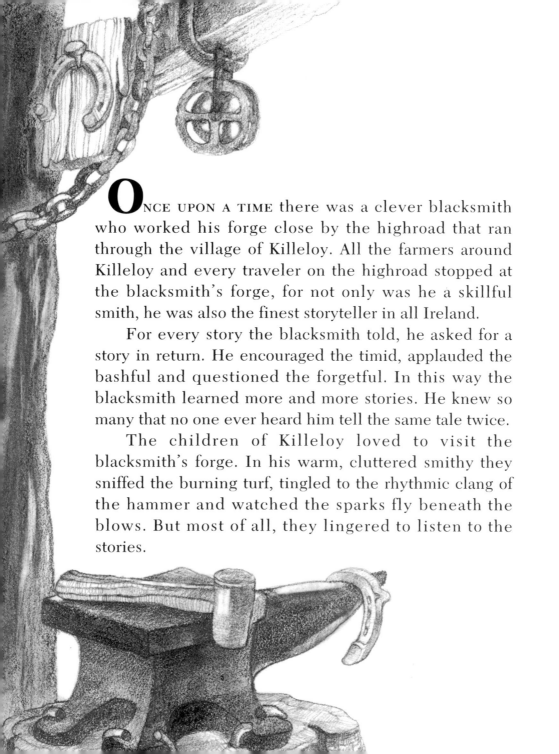

**O**NCE UPON A TIME there was a clever blacksmith who worked his forge close by the highroad that ran through the village of Killeloy. All the farmers around Killeloy and every traveler on the highroad stopped at the blacksmith's forge, for not only was he a skillful smith, he was also the finest storyteller in all Ireland.

For every story the blacksmith told, he asked for a story in return. He encouraged the timid, applauded the bashful and questioned the forgetful. In this way the blacksmith learned more and more stories. He knew so many that no one ever heard him tell the same tale twice.

The children of Killeloy loved to visit the blacksmith's forge. In his warm, cluttered smithy they sniffed the burning turf, tingled to the rhythmic clang of the hammer and watched the sparks fly beneath the blows. But most of all, they lingered to listen to the stories.

One boy of the village, Liam McGowan, who was the blacksmith's own nephew, came every day.

"I want to be a blacksmith, Uncle," Liam declared one day. "I want to be strong and clever, like you."

"You may hold the reins of the horses while I shoe them," the blacksmith replied.

So Liam did.

"I want to be a blacksmith, Uncle," Liam said again some months later. "I want to know the secrets of smithing."

"You may sweep out the forge and fill the water trough," the blacksmith replied.

And every day Liam did.

"I want to be a blacksmith, Uncle," Liam repeated some time later. "I want to make useful and beautiful things."

"You will make a fine blacksmith, Liam," replied his uncle.

So when he was nine years old Liam McGowan was apprenticed to his uncle to learn the blacksmith's trade.

Each morning Liam came early to the smithy. He arranged sods of turf in a tight circle in the forge and sprinkled wood chips in the center. The blacksmith lit the wood chips, and as the fire grew, Liam pumped the bellows, sending a stream of air into the burning turf to make the fire hotter and hotter.

The blacksmith selected a piece of iron suitable for the work at hand and thrust it into the fire. They watched while it heated and grew cherry red. Then the blacksmith drew out the iron with his tongs, laid it on the anvil and began to strike the soft and glowing metal with his hammer. The hammer blows rang and the sparks danced and the iron took on a new shape. Latches and keys, spades and shepherds' crooks, gates, pots, nails— anything made of iron might take form beneath the blacksmith's hammer. To Liam it seemed like magic.

After some months the blacksmith gave Liam a small sledge hammer and Liam worked as a striker. The blacksmith hit the hot iron with his hammer and Liam struck the same spot with the sledge. One after the other, hammer and sledge, the blows fell and something useful and beautiful took shape on the anvil. The blows of the hammer and sledge sounded like music, enchanted music, to Liam. A tap of the blacksmith's hammer on the side of the anvil was a signal for the blows to stop and for talk to begin.

While he set the piece into the fire to reheat, or plunged it into water to cool if it were finished, the blacksmith talked. He explained the work underway, or he questioned and conversed with visitors, or he told stories. This was the best part of all for Liam, who sometimes felt he could listen forever.

Not long after Liam was apprenticed, there came a wild and stormy Halloween day. Few people ventured out on the roads, but Liam McGowan made his way through wind and rain to the blacksmith's forge.

"You are a brave young fellow, Nephew, to come out in such wind and rain," declared the blacksmith. "Not many would do it. Today I will help you make something for yourself, and today I will tell a special story just for you."

"Please, Uncle," replied Liam, "I would like to make something for my mother."

"A splendid idea," said the blacksmith. "Why don't you make her some buckles for her shoes?"

"I would like that fine," answered Liam.

Under the blacksmith's direction, Liam selected a thin iron rod. He heated it in the forge, hammered it, bent it, twisted it three times on each side, and made a pretty iron buckle for his mother's left shoe. He plunged it into the water trough to cool it. Then he set it on the edge of the forge, and he and his uncle admired his handiwork.

"Now, what kind of story would you like me to tell you?" asked the blacksmith.

"You know so many stories, Uncle," said Liam, "but what is your favorite one? That's the one I would like to hear."

"My favorite story? That's a difficult choice to make." The blacksmith considered for a moment. "Now that I think about it, I suppose all my favorite stories are about blacksmiths, good and bad. There have been blacksmiths who were heroes, blacksmiths who were traitors, scholars, and saints. I could tell about Saint Colm or Saint Eloy; both of them were fine smiths. But," he added with a chuckle, "I think I prefer the story of a blacksmith who was a rogue. His name was Will Cooper, but he is remembered as 'Will o' the Wisp'."

"Tell me that story, Uncle. Tell me about Will o' the Wisp."

So the blacksmith told Liam the story of Will Cooper, the blacksmith who outwitted the devil himself, but, because of all his trickery, found the gates of both Heaven and Hell barred against him.

When he finished, Liam was silent for a while. Then he said, "I may forget many things in my life, Uncle, but I will never forget the story of Will o' the Wisp."

"You may make many things at the forge, Liam, but nothing you make will mean more to your mother than the buckle you made for her today. Give it to her," said the blacksmith, "and when you come back tomorrow you can tell me *your* favorite story, and you can make a matching buckle for your mother's right shoe."

"I will," promised Liam.

The next day Liam did not come to the forge. Instead, his father came with the terrible news that Liam was missing. His mother and father and all the villagers searched the countryside for the boy. Day after day they looked. They found no trace of him, except for the pretty iron buckle with three twists on each side that Liam's father found on the highroad.

Days passed, and weeks, and months, and years. Gradually, the search for Liam McGowan ended. His brokenhearted mother and father gave up hope of ever seeing their son again.

But the blacksmith, without leaving the forge, continued to search for the missing boy. He questioned all travelers who came to his forge, listening for a hint, a word, or a suggestion of what might have happened to Liam McGowan.

Seven years passed. Halloween came again. It was a wild and stormy day when few travelers ventured out on the roads. The blacksmith sat idly staring at the glowing coals in the forge. He had no heart for work. His thoughts were on the day seven years before when Liam had disappeared.

A sudden light rap at the door startled him. He was even more surprised when he flung open the door and saw a bent old woman outside. Rain had drenched the black shawl she had wrapped around her head and shoulders, and the wind had reddened her nose and tossed her thin white hair.

"Come in, come in, good woman," urged the smith, and he helped the old woman to a seat beside the fire.

"What are you doing out on such a stormy day?" he asked as he prepared some tea for both of them.

"I am visiting my grandchild who is sick. I have come here to ask for some forge water which, as you know, has healing powers." The old woman took a small empty bottle from under her shawl and set it on the edge of the water trough. "Thank you kindly for the tea, blacksmith," she went on. "It will give me strength to go back through the storm. I must get home before dark. Today is Halloween and strange things happen on this night."

"Aye," agreed the blacksmith. "It reminds me of a Halloween seven years ago." The blacksmith then told the old woman about how his apprentice, his own nephew, had disappeared.

The old woman listened in brooding silence. When the blacksmith ended his tale, she shook her head sadly.

"I heard the same story long, long ago. My mother told it to me. It happened when my mother herself was a child. The blacksmith's apprentice was stolen away on Halloween night."

The blacksmith leaned forward excitedly. "You say the blacksmith's apprentice was stolen. How do you know he was stolen? Who took him? Was he ever found again?"

"A woman who was old and wise when my mother was young and foolish told her that a giant dwells in a cave under the hill of Knockcasur. He comes out, once in a hundred years, on the night when spirits roam—on Halloween—and steals an apprentice to work in his forge. I myself have heard the sound of the giant's hammer striking deep within the hill."

"But if this is true, why did no one go after the boy? Was there no one brave enough to face the giant and claim the child?"

"It was too late, too late they learned the truth," the old woman declared. "And you are too late, if you are thinking of trying to rescue your nephew. Surely you know that if a human spends seven years in the Other World, the world of fairies and pookas and giants, he is lost to this world forever. You are too late."

"No," cried the blacksmith, "it is not too late. He was taken seven years ago today, but the day is not yet over. There may still be time."

Quickly the blacksmith pulled on his coat and cap and flung his largest hammer over his shoulder. "Take the forge water, good woman, and may it bring health to your grandchild," declared the blacksmith, "and thank you for bringing the news for which I have searched for seven years."

"You must be out of the giant's cave before the sun rises or you, too, will be trapped," the old woman warned. "God be between you and all harm," she blessed him, and the blacksmith strode off into the storm toward Knockcasur.

The storm had passed, but darkness was falling when the blacksmith arrived at Knockcasur. In the dim light he saw the hill black with brambles and thickets. At the base of a cliff, which formed the eastern side of the hill, a river gushed from an opening in the bare rock. The blacksmith studied the mouth of the river. This could not be the entrance to the giant's cave, he decided. A full-grown man could barely squeeze through the opening so a giant could never enter there.

In the fading light the blacksmith searched for an entrance. Beneath any tangled mass of bushes, behind any stand of trees, might lie the passageway to the giant's cave.

The moon rose and stars watched from the sky as the blacksmith tramped through brambles, pushed through clumps of thorny trees, poked into hollows and cracks in the hillside.

The moon was high, the night passing quickly, when the blacksmith slumped down upon a rock at the top of the hill to rest and think.

Somewhere there was an entrance to the giant's cave. "But where is it?" he cried out in despair.

The night was still after the storm. Moonlight silvered the trees. Clouds hung unmoving in the sky. Then in that breathless silence the blacksmith heard the whisper of rustling leaves. He looked around expectantly.

A short distance away, leaves trembled on the twisted branches of a blackthorn bush. Yet there was no wind.

The blacksmith rose and approached the quivering leaves. Now he felt a cold draft flow over him. Such a cool rush of air must come from a cave, thought the blacksmith. He tore through a mass of entwined branches, striking them down with his hammer, following the cool current of air to its source, and there it was—the entrance to the giant's cave.

The opening was less than five feet high and perhaps seven feet wide. No doubt the giant has to squeeze to get through here, thought the blacksmith. He bent his head and stepped into the opening. Brambles and branches closed behind him. He felt his way along a twisting tunnel. Light gleamed ahead. He turned a corner and found himself in a huge corridor lit by torches stuck in iron braces here and there high on the rough stone walls.

The blacksmith hurried along the passageway. Down, down he went. In the flickering light of the torches the walls seemed almost alive with grimacing faces. When he looked at the faces, the beard of one became the hair of another. What seemed at first to be a nose of one face, the next moment seemed the ear of its neighbor. At one place in the winding, twisting corridor the blacksmith thought he saw eyes staring at him from the stones. Then he turned a corner and beheld mouths—

laughing, jeering, screaming, horrible mouths. He hurried past them. Water dripped from the ceiling in places and he glimpsed pools and streams in galleries off the corridor. At last the passageway ended before a heavy iron gate. The gate was ajar, and the blacksmith slowly and quietly pushed it open and stepped into an enormous forge.

There was the giant.

He was asleep in an iron chair with his great head resting on an enormous stone table. Behind the giant, coals smoldered in a massive furnace cut into the stone wall. Hammers, sledges, tongs, rasps and all the other tools of a smith were arranged conveniently near his anvil and forge.

The blacksmith looked admiringly around the gigantic room. Ah, what a forge. The ceiling vaulted up a hundred feet or more into the shadows. From a ledge high in the wall, a waterfall cascaded into a river which rushed along one side of the room and disappeared beneath a low arch of rock. The giant cools his work in that river, the blacksmith observed. There were samples of the giant's work piled here and there around the room

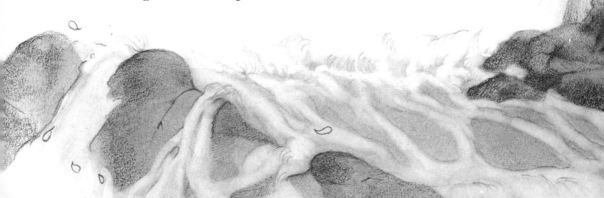

—chains, axes, spears, cauldrons, and horseshoes, hundreds and hundreds of horseshoes of all sizes. The blacksmith picked up a tiny one. The fairy horse this would fit could be no larger than a cat, he thought, and threw it down with a shudder.

Then the blacksmith raised his hammer and with a mighty blow struck the giant's table making a sizable chip in its surface.

"Wake up, you thief," he shouted. "I have come for Liam McGowan."

The giant arose with a start, upsetting the table and shattering it into dozens of pieces no bigger than milk pails.

"Who dares disturb the peace of my house?" roared the giant.

"I am the blacksmith of Killeloy. I have come to claim Liam McGowan."

"By what right do you claim him?" demanded the giant.

"By the right of a master blacksmith. Liam McGowan is my apprentice. He is bound to me for seven years of service."

The giant stepped closer and towered over the blacksmith, who bravely stood his ground.

"I have heard of you, blacksmith of Killeloy. You are reputed to be a great storyteller. I would enjoy hearing a good story. Sit down and tell me a tale or two. There is

plenty of time to get your apprentice."

"First, return Liam McGowan to me," countered the blacksmith. "I want to see the boy so that I can be sure you have done him no harm. Only after that will I tell you a story."

The giant laughed. "Very well, blacksmith. You may
see him." He clapped his huge hands together. The clap
echoed like the rumble of thunder through dark crevasses
and unseen passageways of the cave. A dozen boys came

running to the forge. They were dressed in black knee britches and gray shirts and stockings. They all seemed to be about nine years old.

The blacksmith looked from one to the other. It was seven years since he had seen Liam, but surely he should recognize his own nephew. In the flickering light of the

torches the blacksmith could not see clearly. He rubbed his eyes. Was it a trick the giant played on him or did all the boys look alike? The blacksmith studied each face.

"None of these boys can be Liam McGowan," the blacksmith said at last. Liam McGowan was nine years old seven years ago. He is now a boy of sixteen."

The giant howled with laughter and the boys laughed too.

"Ah, blacksmith, here is a tale you have not heard before. A guest in my kingdom never grows old. Some of these lucky lads have worked as apprentices in my forge for hundreds of years. They could tell you stories worth the hearing."

"And I could tell you stories I have heard," replied the blacksmith, "stories of parents searching for lost children; stories of how they mourned for them."

"These boys can remember nothing of the families they left. Nothing," declared the giant. "They cannot even remember their own names. The parents who wept for them have grown old and died. These children are children forever."

"A mother and father still mourn for Liam McGowan," answered the blacksmith. "And I have come to claim him."

"Your claim means nothing to me," exclaimed the giant, "but I long to hear a good story; so I will make a bargain with you. You may have your apprentice in exchange for a story. But take care, blacksmith, that you choose correctly," warned the giant. "If you pick the wrong boy, then you forfeit your claim to him and you, too, must stay here with me forever. Choose. Then tell us a story."

The blacksmith looked closely at the twelve boys. They seemed identical in every way. He strained his eyes, but he could not see them clearly in the sputtering,

flickering torchlight. Shadows danced on their laughing faces. Their features blurred before his eyes. Though these boys do not remember their own names, they may have other memories, the blacksmith thought.

"Gather around me, lads. First, I will pick out Liam McGowan. Then I will tell a grand story you have not heard before, the story of Will o' the Wisp," promised the blacksmith.

"Good. Good. Please do," all the boys shouted.

Except for one, who said quietly, "But I have heard that story before."

"This is Liam McGowan," cried the blacksmith, and he grasped the hand of the boy who had just spoken.

"Yes, yes, I am Liam McGowan," the boy exclaimed. "I can remember now. Take me away from here, Uncle."

"We must get out of this cave before sunrise or we will be trapped," whispered the blacksmith. "Stay close to me." Hand in hand they moved toward the gate through which the blacksmith had entered the giant's forge.

"My story," roared the giant. "You cannot leave until you tell me a story. That was the bargain."

"There is no time for a story now," answered the blacksmith. "Come to my forge and I will tell you a story. It was not part of the bargain that I should tell it here."

"You think you have tricked me, but you shall never leave here," thundered the giant. In a bound he crossed the room, slammed shut the iron gate and turned to seize the blacksmith.

Before the huge cruel hands could close upon him, the blacksmith hurled his hammer with all his might and struck the giant on the forehead. The giant staggered back with a terrible cry, knocking over columns of stone as he fell with his back against the iron gate.

"Quick, Liam, is there another way out? Where do these passageways lead?" asked the blacksmith.

"To other rooms, to other chambers, Uncle. The only way out lies behind that gate."

The giant was now on his knees. He was rising to his feet. "You will never leave here, blacksmith." He lunged toward the terrified pair.

"The river, Liam, That's a way out. Hold tight to my jacket," cried the blacksmith, and they plunged into the churning river.

The force of the rushing water swept them through the low archway into the narrow channel the river had cut through the stone. The giant was in the river after them. He stretched in his arm through the archway and grasped Liam's heel. Liam shook his foot and his wet shoe slipped off in the giant's hand. The blacksmith and Liam were beyond the giant's reach.

"You owe me a story," they heard the giant shout after them.

They half-swam, half-waded through the icy water that pushed them along. There was scarcely enough room between the top of the water and the roof of the cave for them to breathe. Soon the cave narrowed to a small, low tunnel through which the river flowed right to the roof.

"This tunnel leads to the outside, Liam. We are almost free. You must hold your breath now." Liam took a deep breath, and the blacksmith gave him a strong push, sending him out through the tunnel.

The blacksmith took a deep breath as well and followed, pushing, squeezing, inching his way through the narrow opening. He tried to grasp the slippery rock to pull himself along, but the space was too small. He could go no farther. He was trapped in the tunnel.

At that moment the blacksmith felt Liam's hand grasp his. With all the strength he had developed at the giant's forge, Liam gave a mighty pull, and the blacksmith was out.

Uncle and nephew lay gasping and exhausted by the bank of the river. They lay there while the last stars faded in the sky and the calling of the birds announced the coming of dawn. Then uncle and nephew got up and walked hand in hand to Liam's home.

Liam's mother answered the door. She saw her son, fell to her knees and hugged him to her breast.

But Liam's father hung back. "What kind of cruel trick is this?" he asked the blacksmith. "This child is like our son was seven years ago, but our son would now be sixteen years of age."

The blacksmith told them of the boys whom the giant had stolen hundreds of years before, who were still children.

But Liam's father was not sure.

"Come to the forge," said the blacksmith. "Liam can prove to you that he is your son."

At the forge, the blacksmith said, "Liam, finish your mother's present."

Liam McGowan took a thin rod of iron, and with fire and hammer and anvil he fashioned a pretty buckle with three twists on each side for his mother's right shoe.

His father watched in amazement and delight. "Welcome home, Liam, my son."

"Well now," declared the blacksmith happily, "if the giant ever comes to the forge to claim his story, I will tell him one with the ending he didn't expect—the story of how Liam McGowan came home."

Liam grew to be a strong and clever man and became, in his turn, a master blacksmith. It was said that he never forgot the secrets of iron smithing he had learned at the giant's forge. Travelers from all over Ireland stopped at the forge to see his marvelous work and to hear him tell again the story of when he was the giant's apprentice.